Agatha Parrot

AND THE Odd Street School Ghost

Agatha Parrot

AND THE Odd Street School Ghost

TYPED OUT NEATLY BY
KJARTAN POSKITT

ILLUSTRATED BY
WES HARGIS

CLARION BOOKS
HOUGHTON MIFFLIN HARCOURT
BOSTON NEW YORK

Library of Congress Cataloging-in-Publication Data is available.
ISBN 978-0-544-50672-5

Manufactured in the United States of America
DOC 10 9 8 7 6 5 4 3 2 1
4500598718

This book is dedicated to Tony,
who's my hero, because without him
this story would have had a
really rotten ending. xxx

THE GANG!

Ivy always says hello when she sees herself in mirrors.

Agatha (that's me). There are wet things with eyes and legs living in the bottom of my schoolbag. And that's true.

Ellie is scared of nonfat milk because she thinks it comes from skeleton cows.

Contents

How to Read This Book

Hiya!

Have you ever been woken up by a ghost? I have!

Actually, it wasn't the ghost that woke me up; it was the bell in our school clock, but this story does have a ghost in it, so be prepared to be scared— *WOOO!*—fear, fear, tremble!

If you want to see where the bell is, look at the pages in the front of this book. You'll see a picture of Odd Street School, which is at the end of the street where I live with my friends. Our street is called Odd Street because the houses just have odd numbers like 1, 3, 5, 7, 9, 11, 13, 15 . . . and so on. If there were any houses on the other side of the street, then they would be the even numbers, but there aren't any.

My name is Agatha Jane Parrot and I live in house number 5, which has a red front door if you want to color it in.

Our school has an old clock tower, and the bell lives inside it, along with some smelly pigeons. The bell is supposed to go *DONG!* at one o'clock and *DONG! DONG!* at two o'clock and *DONG! DONG! DONG!* at three o'clock and so on. But one DARK and STORMY night, things got very strange, so get ready for some spooky goings-on!

Here are some tips on how to read a ghost book:

1) Make sure you're sitting with your back to the wall. That way, nobody can creep up behind you and make you jump, which is what my evil brother, James, always tries to do. He's just SO predictable.

2) Don't read this book in the dark, because that would be REALLY scary! Er . . . no, it wouldn't, because if it was dark, you wouldn't be able to read it. Forget this one.

3) Make sure you've got a tennis racket handy, so if a person in a white sheet comes past going *Wooo* (i.e., James again), you can give them a

good WHACK! The best thing about this is that if it turns out to be a real ghost, the tennis racket will go right through it and slice it into ghost fries—ha ha! Actually, I'm not sure if that would work, but it has to be worth a try.

All right, good luck! Off we go . . .

Midnight Chimes

It was a DARK AND STORMY NIGHT on Odd Street.

Woo woo woo went the wind. *Whoosh whoosh whoosh* went the rain on the windows.

Up in the tiny back bedroom of house number 5, a very charming and lovely girl* with crazy hair and awesome freckles was trying to get to sleep.

*(That's me, if you hadn't guessed.)

Actually, I wasn't trying very hard to get to sleep, because I LOVE stormy nights, but I could hardly hear any of it because of all the other noises in our house.

To start with, I had my little sister, Tilly, sleeping on the bottom bunk underneath me, going *Snore snore snore*. As well as that, Dad was sitting downstairs watching the TV — *blah-dee blah blah* — the washing machine was going *rum-shloppa rum-shloppa*, and Mom was on the phone to her friend Alice going *Yabber yabber yabber oh, really? Yabber yabber I told you so yabber yabber HA HA HA serves him right! Yabber yabber.*

I still managed to get to sleep, because the only noise that ever kept me awake was when James used to practice with his soccer ball against his bedroom wall. *BUDDUNK BUDDUNK BUDDUNK* CRASH! Luckily Mom told him that if he ever did it again, she'd burn his soccer shoes and make him take piano lessons, so that was the end of that, THANK GOODNESS.

So a little wind and rain was never going to keep me awake for long. Off I went to sleepy-peeps, but then what DID wake me up was when it got all quiet. The wind and rain had stopped, Mom and Dad had gone to bed, and Tilly had rolled over and stopped making noises. All of a sudden I was wide awake again, staring at the ceiling. Everything was deadly silent, and that's when I find it really spooky! You know the feeling: all you can do is lie there listening for tiny sounds, like a skeleton tapping on the window or a snake hissing under the bed. EEEEK!

I was just getting to sleep again when suddenly . . .

DONG!

It was the bell in the school clock.

DONG!

It was the bell again.

DONG!

That's the trouble with clocks. You can't help . . .

DONG!

. . . but count how many times the . . .

DONG!

. . . bell chimes. And another thing . . .

DONG!

. . . our old bell doesn't always chime at the same speed. Just when you think it's finished, it chimes again . . .

. . . but sometimes it doesn't. So anyway, I had counted six *DONG*s, which meant it was probably six o' —

DONG! DONG!

. . . eight o'clock . . .

DONG!

. . . and this book would get very boring if we

wrote all the *DONG*s out, but altogether I counted twenty-seven of them. If every *DONG* counted for one hour going past, then by my calculations, the clock had *DONG*ed right around until it was three o'clock the next afternoon. That meant it was time to go home from school and I'd missed the spelling test we were going to have. WAHOO!

Good old clock. No wonder I went straight back to sleep with a smile on my face. (Although I couldn't see the smile, of course, because I was asleep.) (And it was dark.) (And it was my own face and I didn't have a mirror, so I couldn't have seen it anyway.) (This is getting silly—ha ha!) (Sausage pie.) (Just thought I'd put that in for no reason!) (I bet the printers take it out.) (The meanies.)

Dad's Smelly Surprise

The next morning I was woken by the soft rays of golden sunlight shining in through the window, the gentle twittering of birds, the smell of bacon, and a giant plasma TV on the wall showing my favorite cartoons.

That would have been nice, wouldn't it? Actually that's a little dream I was having. What really happened was Mom shouting from the kitchen: "AGATHA COME ON GET UP YOU'RE GOING TO BE LATE YOU SHOULD BE GETTING YOUR SHOES ON AND YOU HAVEN'T EVEN EATEN BREAKFAST AND WHAT ABOUT THOSE SPELLING WORDS YOU WERE SUPPOSED TO HAVE LEARNED COME ON AGATHA NOW AGATHA COME ON!"

Ho-hum. So much for the smell of giant birds and the twittering bacon or whatever it was that I'd been dreaming about.

When I got to the kitchen, everybody was sitting around the table. Tilly and James were already eating toast, and Mom was eating some sort of healthy nutty yogurt gunk. I plonked myself into a chair and then saw Dad grinning at me.

"What's up with you?" he asked. "You look awful."

"The school bell kept ringing last night," I said. "Didn't you hear it?"

"No, but never mind," said Dad. "This'll get you going!"

He went to the cabinet and pulled out a big box. It was dark blue with a picture of a bright green fish on it. Mom gave it a funny look.

"What's that?" I asked her.

"I have no idea," she said. "I sent him out to get some breakfast cereal yesterday, and this is what he brought back."

"Looks good, doesn't it?" said Dad proudly.

"NO!" we all said.

"But it was on special sale at Spendless," said Dad.

URGH! That explained it.

Spendless is the shop where my friend Martha's

mom works, and it's full of weird stuff you've never heard of. Mom's always telling Dad not to buy their special sale items, but he never listens.

"Are you sure it's cereal?" I asked him.

"Of course," Dad said, passing the box over to me. "It's called Fishpopz! The new healthy way to start your day."

I opened it up and sniffed inside. Sure enough, it smelled fishy, but with a bit of wet dog in there too.

"Help yourself," said Dad, getting the bowls out. "Fish is very good for you."

"I can smell it from here," said Mom, wrinkling her nose. "What else did you get?"

"You DID get something else, didn't you, Dad?" we said.

"Er . . ." said Dad sheepishly.

"He's only teasing," said Mom. "I saw him coming in with lots of bags. Look in the cabinet, Agatha."

So I looked. OH, NO! There were more dark blue boxes.

"Like I said," explained Dad, "it was on special sale. Buy one, get four free. Come on, let's try it!"

Dad poured some Fishpopz into a bowl. They were little gray fishy shapes, and when he poured the milk in, the milk turned a little gray too.

"Would you rather have toast, Agatha?" asked Mom.

"Yes, please," I said. "But go ahead, Dad, eat your breakfast!"

Dad stared at the gray fish floating around inside his bowl while we had LOVELY toast—ha ha!

Eventually he stuck a spoon in and took a mouthful.

We were all staring at him chewing, so he put a big smile on his face. "You should try some," he said. "Really, it's nice!"

He stuck his spoon into the bowl again, but he was still chewing, so he wasn't ready for the next load yet.

"Let's see you swallow it, Dad," said James.

"Mmm . . . mm," said Dad, who was still chewing, and chewing, and making faces, and chewing. Suddenly he got up and left the kitchen.

"What's silly Daddy doing?" demanded Tilly.

"I'm just getting something," said Dad from the hallway with his mouth still full.

"Liar!" said James, jumping to his feet. "He's going to spit it out in the bathroom."

We all charged out and caught Dad sneaking upstairs.

"You don't all need to come along too," said Dad, still chewing.

"Oh, yes, we do!" we shouted.

HA HA HA!

Sure enough, Dad ended up with his head over the toilet, and it served him RIGHT.

"We'll have to throw the rest away," said James.

"That's a waste of money," moaned Mom.

"Maybe we could put it out for the birds?" I suggested.

"We could NOT," said Mom. "I don't want them dropping dead all over the yard."

"So what can we do with it?" asked Tilly.

It was a very good question.

Hmmmm.

The Boy with Cheese and Onion Hair

The next important thing happened in school at lunchtime.

At this point, my lovely reader, allow me to introduce my friends and their lunches with points out of ten for interestingness.

1) Ivy Malting = cheese sandwich and plain chips (1/10). A boring lunch, but Ivy isn't boring at

all—it's just that she can't have anything with bright colors on it. One sniff of pink icing and she starts jumping on the tables. WAHOO! GO, IVY! We love Ivy.

2) Bianca Bayuss = nutty brown bread thing with olives (9/10). If you think her lunch is weird, that's nothing. Her mom and dad light candles and read gloomy poetry to each other AND . . .

they don't have a TV! No wonder Bianca spends all her evenings playing her trombone like this: *BWARB WAB BARP.*

3) Ellie Slippin = some grapes and two cookies (4/10). Ellie can't eat sandwiches because she feels sorry for the bread that gets sliced up by a big machine full of horrible knives. In Ellie's magic world, bread would have little legs and

eyes and be allowed to play outside. I have to say, I agree with her. Good one, Ellie.

4) Martha Swan = lots and lots of sandwiches (6/10). Martha is big and hearty, and she DOES like her sandwiches! They help her fill the time between meals.

We have lunch in the school cafeteria, but when we arrived, there were only three chairs left for the five of us. I had to share with Ivy, Bianca shared with Ellie, and Martha got a chair to herself. Martha can't really share a chair because (how can I put this politely?) if we were all grapes, then she'd be a melon.

It turned out that I wasn't the only one who had heard the school bell ringing the night before.

"I counted twenty-seven rings," I said.

"I counted twenty-eight," said Ellie.

"Did you count them, Bianca?" I asked.

"No," said Bianca, shaking her head. "It went on loo tong."

"Loo tong?" we said.

"I know what she means," said Ellie. "It went on TOO LONG!"

Ha ha! We love Bianca. We don't always understand her, but we do always love her.

"Bianca's right," said Martha. "I counted sixteen, but then I got bored."

"I counted thirty," said Ivy. "So I win!"

"No, you don't," we all said. "It's not a competition."

"Let's try to stay awake tonight and count the rings," I said. "I hope it does it again."

"Oh, no!" said Ellie, shaking. "I hope it doesn't! The bell ringing gave me a bad dream."

"A bad dream?" I asked. "Why was it bad?"

"Because it was a ghost ringing the bell, and the ghost was making all the hours and days and years fly past at once, and when we woke up, we had all turned into little old ladies."

HA HA HA . . . oh!

We were all laughing, but then Miss Barking came by, and suddenly it wasn't funny anymore.

She's the vice principal. She's got glasses like TV screens, and she wears hairy clothes, and she thinks everything in the world is unsafe. None of us wanted to turn into HER.

Miss B. stared at us all squashed onto our three

chairs. Then she pulled some leaflets out of the big fat folder she always carries.

"That is *not* how we sit on chairs," she said crossly, and plonked the leaflets down in front of us. The leaflets said HOW TO SIT ON A CHAIR in great

big letters, and underneath them was an emergency phone number in case you fell off.

"School chairs should have seat belts," she said. "I keep asking for them, but does anyone ever listen?"

Honestly! Whoever heard of seat belts on chairs? We all looked at one another, thinking the same thing. We *definitely* didn't want to turn into Miss Barking.

When she left, I quickly changed the subject to something a little happier. "Has anyone heard of Fishpopz?" I said.

"I have," said Martha. "They're in Mom's shop. They're so horrible, they had to put them on special sale. What kind of fool would buy a breakfast cereal that tastes of fish?"

I must have made a face, because they all looked at me, then burst out laughing.

"Your dad did, didn't he!" said Martha. "So did you try them?"

"I did not!" I said. "But Dad did. Then he had to go and spit them out in the toilet."

Just then Motley, the school custodian, came past. He had a black trash bag and was putting all the old cookie wrappers and drink cartons in it. He picked up a piece of squashed sandwich and stared at it.

"Waste of good food," he muttered to himself. "It's still got a bit of ham in there. Honestly, kids today!"

He dropped it in his bag, then moved on. But suddenly there was a deafening *BLAPP!*

On the other side of the cafeteria, Danny Frost was looking very cross. He'd been eating a bag of potato chips when his brother, Jake, had come up behind him. Jake had blown up an empty chip bag and then smashed it right by Danny's ear. Danny had jumped out of his skin and spilled his chips all over himself. HA HA! Actually, you shouldn't laugh at boys—it only encourages them.

Danny came stomping over to Motley, dropping chips everywhere. He threw his bag in Motley's bigger trash bag, but he didn't realize he still had a big chip stuck in his hair! We all got the giggles.

"What are you laughing at?" asked Danny.

"Nothing," we said.

That's when Motley reached over and pulled the chip out of Danny's hair.

"Is that the new fashion?" asked Ivy. "Cheese and onion hair?"

"Yum!" said Martha, and we all laughed.

Danny stomped off, leaving Motley holding the

big chip. He was about to drop it in his bag when he sniffed it and then . . . he ate it!

"He ate a chip from Danny's hair?" Ellie gasped.

"Motley eats *anything!*" said Martha admiringly.

"Oooh!" I said. "I wonder if that includes Fishpopz?"

The Haunted Coatroom

The next morning we were all outside the school waiting for Motley to unlock the doors. I had a great big bag to give him, full of you-know-what!

We had all managed to stay awake the night before. I had counted thirty-five *DONG*s. Martha counted thirty-two, Bianca and Ellie both counted thirty-six, and Ivy said she counted twenty million

*DONG*s, the big fibber. But whatever the number was, it was TOO MANY *DONG*s.

"I'm feeling very old," said Ellie. "The time is rushing past!"

"Don't worry about it," said Martha. "They'll get the clock fixed, and then it'll be all right."

"But what if they can't fix it?" said Ellie. "What if my dream was right and it IS a ghost ringing the bell?"

Poor Ellie was shaking a bit, so we all gave her a big team hug.

Unfortunately we didn't know that Gwendoline Tutt had been standing

right behind us and listening. She's the one who lives in the big fancy house at the far end of Odd Street, and she's really horrible.

"Hey, listen to this, everybody!" Gwendoline shouted across the playground. "Ellie Slippin thinks there's a ghost!"

Everybody ignored her except Olivia Livid. Olivia always joins in when Gwendoline is being nasty, so she ran up to Ellie, flapping her arms around.

"WOOO!" shouted Olivia. "WOOO! I'm a ghost!"

Ellie covered her eyes so she couldn't see.

"Little scared Ellie, knees turned to jelly!" sneered Gwendoline. "Imagine being scared of ghosts! There's no such thing."

"How do you know?" demanded Martha.

"Yeah, maybe Ellie's right!" said Ivy. "Maybe there IS a ghost."

"A ghost?" said Gwendoline. "Don't be pathetic."

"Why not?" said Ivy. "It's an old school, so it could be the ghost of an old teacher or something."

"WOOO! I'm a ghost!" went Gwendoline and Olivia together.

Ellie was getting really upset, but then Motley opened the doors. Gwendoline and Olivia rushed inside, but we all hung back so Ellie could get her head together. It gave me the chance to pass the bag to Motley.

"Here's a present for you," I said.

"Me?" said Motley. "What is it?"

"Guess!" I said.

Motley opened the big bag and stuck his nose in. I was standing as far away as I could, but the fishy wet-dog smell was worse than ever!

"If you don't want it, that's fine," I said. "I'll just throw it away."

I reached out to take it, but Motley wouldn't let go.

"Oh, no!" he said. "I hate to see good food wasted."

He stuck his head in the bag again and took another sniff.

"Oh, no," he said again. "You can't throw this out."

And off he went, down to his secret room, which I'll tell you about later.

We went to the coatroom to hang our coats up.

There were some sinks at the far end, so Ellie went to splash a little water on her face to make herself feel better. Gwendoline was hanging around outside, and we ignored her, but when we came out, she said, "Hey, Ellie Jelly-Knees! You must be right about that ghost. Look, it threw your gloves on the floor."

Ellie looked back. Sure enough, her gloves were lying underneath her coat.

"They were in my pocket!" said Ellie.

"Gwendoline pulled them out," said Martha crossly.

"I was nowhere near them," said Gwendoline. "It must be a ghostly hand crawling around!"

Ellie was shivering a bit.

"She's just being stupid," said Martha. "Ignore her."

Ellie took a deep breath to be brave, then went to pick her gloves up. Just as she was tucking them back into her pocket, the sleeve of the coat next to her started moving. It reached up, and then a hand came out of the end and grabbed Ellie's arm.

"ARGH!" shrieked Ellie.

Martha stomped over and pulled the coat off the peg. Olivia was hiding behind it.

"WOOO! I'm a ghost!" Olivia sneered.

"That was NOT funny," said Martha.

"Oh, yes, it was!" Gwendoline sniggered. "Honestly, you guys are SO pathetic. Imagine believing in ghosts! We're going to tell everyone."

Ghost Fever

Poor Ellie. She spent the morning trying to forget about ghosts, but at recess the whole school was talking about them. Even the little kiddies were running up behind people and shouting, "WOOO! I'm a ghost!"

Little kids are fabulous because they don't understand the meaning of danger. Miss Barking was on playground duty, and as usual there was a big mess around the trash cans, so as usual she said, "Who made all this mess?"

"It was the ghost!" screamed all the kiddies, and then they made ghostie faces and shouted "WOOO!" and ran off.

Awesome! If I'd done that, Miss Barking would be screaming mad, but of course she can't be screaming mad around the kiddies in case they wet themselves. All she could do was look in her folder for a leaflet about ghosts, and then when she couldn't find one, she stomped inside to sulk— ha ha!

Everybody thought it was really funny except Ellie, but then I saw something to cheer her up. Jake Frost had taken Danny over to the main entrance and was daring him to push the button for the door buzzer and go "WOOO!" into the intercom. Danny was giggling, but I knew he was scared. I didn't blame him!

If you don't think this sounds very exciting, then you've never met Miss Wizzit. She's our school receptionist, and she is NOT a happy little ray of sunshine. She hates cars parked in the wrong place, she hates wet umbrellas in the hall, she hates the phone ringing when she's secretly painting her toenails under her desk (I know because I caught her doing it once—ha ha!), but most of all she DOUBLE HATES people playing with the door buzzer.

"Come on, Ellie," I said. "Let's get inside and see what happens."

"We can't just go and spy on Miss Wizzit!" said
Ellie.

"Of course we can," I said. I put my arm around
Ellie's shoulders so she could hold me up, and then
I started limping toward the back door. "If anybody
asks, I've just twisted my knee."

Ellie helped me hobble into the office, where we saw Miss Wizzit standing on a chair. She was trying to pin a calendar to the wall, so obviously Danny hadn't been brave enough to push the buzzer yet.

We sat down, and then I moaned and groaned a bit while Ellie pretended to rub my knee better. If there's one thing you can rely on, it's that the more fuss you make, the more Miss Wizzit will ignore you, which is exactly what we wanted.

She slipped off her shoe and was using it to hammer a thumbtack when the front door buzzer went *BZZZzZZzzzZ.*

She got down and put the tack on the chair, then pushed the button on her desk. She was still holding her shoe with the other hand. "Wizzit?" said Miss Wizzit.

"WOOO!" said Danny's voice.

"Who?" said Miss Wizzit.

"No," said Danny. "WOOO."

"WHO?" demanded Miss Wizzit, giving her shoe an angry shake.

"WOOO! It's the GHOST!"

Miss Wizzit dashed over to the door and pulled it open. Danny and Jake were running off, so without thinking, she hurled her shoe after them, then slammed the door shut—*WHAM!*

Then she looked down and saw her bare foot with five little toes wiggling at her.

"GRRRR!" said Miss Wizzit.

She yanked the door open again and went hopping across the playground to rescue her shoe.

Ellie was the happiest I'd seen her all day. "Miss

Wizzit throwing her shoe away is the BEST thing I've ever seen in my WHOLE LIFE!" She giggled.

When Miss Wizzit came back in, we were rubbing my knee and pretending not to watch her and trying not to laugh all at the same time, but then it got even better!

Miss Barking came in just as Miss Wizzit was getting back up on her chair. "I hope you're not going to climb on that chair, Miss Wizzit!"

"Why not?" snapped Miss Wizzit.

"The only thing that's safe to climb is a ladder," said Miss Barking.

"But you've locked the ladder up!" snapped Miss Wizzit.

"I know," said Miss Barking. She jangled her keys and looked very pleased with herself. "That way nobody can climb it, so now it's even safer."

"A chair is safe enough," said Miss Wizzit.

"Chairs are only safe for sitting on," said Miss B., and then she reached into her fat folder and pulled out one of her HOW TO SIT ON A CHAIR leaflets and waved it in Miss Wizzit's face.

"Allow me to demonstrate," said Miss Barking, and then she sat down, right on Miss Wizzit's thumbtack.

"YOW!" she yelped, and jumped up again. "Who left that tack there?" she demanded, rubbing her bottom crossly.

Miss Wizzit gave her a long stare. Then an evil smile came to her face.

"It was the ghost," said Miss Wizzit. "WOOO."

Ellie was laughing so much, it was ME that had to hold HER up when we walked back to the classroom!

The Mysterious Window

By the time Ellie and me got to class, we were a little bit late, but it was okay because our teacher is Miss Pingle, who we like a LOT. She's a new teacher and about one hundred years younger than the other teachers, and she's got groovy hair that changes color every week. (This week's color = emerald green. She said it was deep and rich like her personality, but we thought it made her head look like a giant pea — ha ha!)

Miss Pingle didn't notice me and Ellie sneaking in because the window had come open. It's really high up and the class was getting cold, so Miss P. was being EXTREMELY NAUGHTY. She had climbed onto a table to shut it (gasp, shock, horror — how wicked!), but she was nowhere near high enough.

"That's not how to do it," I said.

"So what am I supposed to do?" asked Miss P.

"You have to guard the door," I said. "Then Ivy climbs up."

"Ivy?" said Miss Pingle.

"Ivy," we said.

Before Miss Pingle could say anything, Ivy had

jumped onto a desk and then walked over two more to get to the tall shelves. Ivy is an expert. When we were little kiddies in Miss Bunn's class, Miss Bunn was always busy helping the other kiddies with their paintings, so when she wasn't looking, Ivy used to practice climbing all the way around the room without touching the floor. The only time it went wrong was when she slipped on the edge of the sink. She ended up sitting in the water and had to go and get some dry tights and undies from Miss Wizzit's "little accident" cabinet! Good times.

In our class there's a water pipe running near the top of the wall that Ivy needed to swing along, and the tricky part for Ivy was reaching out from the shelves to grab it. If Ivy fell off, she'd have landed on the computer, so watching her took nerves of steel.

Unfortunately Miss P. didn't have nerves of steel.

"Ivy, get down!" she said. "I'll shut the window."

"But you have to keep watch by the door," I said.

"Don't be silly," said Miss P. "I'm the teacher, for goodness' sake! I'm not keeping watch for Ivy."

Ivy got down, and then Miss Pingle tried again. She got one of the small tables and put it on the table by the window. Then she put a chair on top of it. We were so busy watching her climb up that we didn't notice the classroom door open.

"Miss Pingle!" shrieked Miss Barking. "You're supposed to be a teacher, NOT a monkey!"

Miss Pingle climbed down and put the chair and table back on the floor. It was really embarrassing for her, so we all pretended to be reading and doing our work.

"If you need to shut that window, you must use the ladder," said Miss Barking.

"I'll go get it," said Miss Pingle.

"You can't," said Miss Barking. "I've locked it up so people can't use it."

"But that's silly," said Miss Pingle.

Miss Barking hissed angrily.

(Me and Ellie weren't surprised that she was in such a bad mood. She probably still had a sore bottom from sitting on Miss Wizzit's thumbtack!)

Miss Barking took Miss Pingle out into the hall, and we could hear her scolding Miss P. for climbing on the furniture. Of course, as soon as they were gone, Martha went to keep watch at the door, and Ivy was back on the shelves, leaping across to grab the pipe.

By the time Miss Pingle came back into the classroom, we were all back in our seats being good little children.

Miss Barking stuck her head through the door. "Remember what I said. That window will stay open until . . . EH?"

She looked up and saw that the window was shut.

"How did that happen?" she said.

We all looked up and GASPED and pretended

it was a big surprise. Ivy even fell off her chair and fainted onto the floor in shock—ha ha!

Miss Barking looked around suspiciously, but we were all at our desks, there were no chairs and tables piled up, and of course it would have been quite impossible for any of us nice little people to reach that window.

"I don't understand," said Miss Barking. "Did anyone see what happened?"

Nobody said anything, so Miss Barking walked around, giving us all scary stares. She stopped next to Ellie because she knew Ellie was the easiest person to frighten. Poor Ellie was shivering in fear, but I knew she wouldn't let us down.

"Maybe . . . maybe it was the ghost," said Ellie.

GOOD ONE, ELLIE!

"WOOO! It's the ghost!" said everybody.

"There is NO ghost!" snapped Miss Barking, but then she looked up at the high window again and rubbed her sore bottom. "Is there?"

Miss Barking went away looking very worried.

Of course Miss Pingle knew exactly what had happened.

"Ivy Malting, come here."

Ivy walked up to the front. Miss Pingle was making her really serious face.

"I want you to tell that ghost never to touch my windows again! Do you understand?"

"Yes, Miss Pingle," said Ivy.

"Oh, and Ivy?" said Miss P.

"What?" said Ivy.

"Tell the ghost I said thank you."

A big cheer and a round of applause for Miss Pingle—WAHOO! Clap, clap, clap!

She is just SO cool.

The Bell and the
Bipper Sloots

That night, the bell went bonkers.

DONG! DONG! DONG! DONG! and
DONG! DONG! DONG!

It must have rung about a hundred *DONG*s
when I heard Mom get up and go downstairs, so
I went to find her. She was in the kitchen wearing
her nightie and having a glass of water.

"I wish they'd fix that bell," she said.

"Ellie says a ghost is ringing it," I told her.

"Well, I wish he'd stop it," said Mom.

Then we heard some voices out on the sidewalk. I looked through the curtains and saw it was Martha and Ivy with their moms. They had their coats on over their nightclothes and were talking about the bell, but then guess who came running down the street to join them?

It was Ellie! I never thought she'd be out at night, especially with all those spooky *DONG*s going on.

"I'm going out too," I said.

"No, you are not," said Mom.

Then Dad stuck his head in through the kitchen door.

"Come on, Agatha!" he said. "Let's go out and see what's going on."

Good old Dad! I dashed to the hall and got my coat on.

Mom gave in and followed me. She took a good look at Dad. He was wearing his old raincoat, and underneath it he had on his ratty bedtime T-shirt and shorts, plus . . . on his feet he had Mom's woolly

slipper boots, which had knitted eyes and little ears sticking out of them!

"We won't be long," said Dad.

"Be as long as you like," said Mom rudely. "I'm in no rush to see anyone coming home dressed like that."

As soon as we stepped outside, Ivy ran up and gave me a big hug.

"It's AGATHA!" she shouted.

"Shhh, child of mine!" said Ivy's mom. "If you shout like that in the night, you'll wake the dead."

Martha's mom looked at Dad and giggled. "It looks like one of the dead is already awake!" she said.

"WOOO!" said me and Martha.

The bell was still *DONG*ing, so we walked down to the school gates.

As we went past number 1, Bianca came out with her mom and dad, which was great because Bianca's dad always seems sort of serious. Not tonight! He had slipper boots on exactly the same as my dad did.

"Snap!" they both said, waving their feet at each other.

"It's embarrassing when your dad wears your mom's slipper boots, isn't it?" I whispered to Bianca.

"It's worse for me," said Bianca. "Dad isn't wearing Mom's bipper sloots. Those are HIS bipper sloots."

"Bipper sloots?" we all said.

"She means slipper boots!" Ellie giggled.

HA HA HA HA!

I was really glad that Ellie's mom had let her come out. Being with us was a lot more fun for her than worrying about the bell, especially when Bianca's dad brought out some drinks, and Martha's mom fetched a giant box of cookies! It's hard to be scared when you're having a midnight picnic in the street along with two men wearing bipper sloots.

We were all having so much fun that it was a long time before we realized the bell had stopped.

"It's just resting," said Martha. "It does that. It'll ring again soon."

"Let's all hold our breath until it rings," said Ivy.

So me and Ivy and Martha and Bianca and Ellie held our breath until the next *DONG*. And we waited and we waited . . .

"Oh, my!" said Ivy's mom, and she pointed up at the school. "Will you look at that!"

Something was glowing in the top corner of one of the upstairs windows.

"It's a reflection," said Bianca's dad. "The moon or something."

But there wasn't any moon in the sky that night.

Besides, the thing in the window was more of a green color.

"It looks like a face," said Martha. "And it's horrible."

"There's somebody in there!" Dad gasped. "We'd better phone the police."

"But it's glowing," said Ivy.

"And it's far too high up for a normal person," I said.

As we watched, the face started to drift down and sway from side to side.

Ivy giggled. "I know what it is!" she said. "It's a balloon."

"A balloon with a face?"

"Remember that time we made a dummy to look

like Martha? We got a yellow balloon and drew a face on it to make the head."

We all decided Ivy must be right. Somebody must have made a green balloon head and left it floating around the school.

But then the face turned even more horrible and the mouth opened.

"That's not a balloon!" said Martha.

"Then what is it?" said Ivy.

From up in the school, we heard the sound of a distant groan . . . "Arghhh!"

"I was right all along!" shrieked Ellie. "THERE *IS* A GHOST!"

EEEKY FREAK!

Mrs. Twelvetrees Has a Brilliant Idea

"I shall say this for the VERY last and FINAL time," said Mrs. Twelvetrees. "There is NO ghost at Odd Street School!"

It was the next day, and Mrs. Twelvetrees had called everyone into the auditorium for a special assembly. Mrs. Twelvetrees is our principal, who is very hearty and sporty and marches around in big sensible shoes—*stomp stomp stomp*. We don't normally have special assemblies, but Mrs. T. had to do something because everybody had heard about

what we had seen, and the whole school was totally spooked out!

Martha put her hand up. "What was that green face we saw last night, in that case?" she asked.

"And we're not lying," said Ivy, waving her hand in the air. "Our moms and dads saw it too."

"Oooh!" said everybody. They all sounded jealous, especially the boys!

It was kind of cool, actually.

"Humph," said Mrs. Twelvetrees. She looked cross. "Anybody who thinks they saw this ghost, put your hand up."

Me and Ellie and Martha and Ivy and Bianca all put our hands up.

"You too, Bianca?" said Mrs. Twelvetrees. "You're normally quite sensible."

"It was scary." Bianca nodded earnestly. "It made my wees go knobbly."

HA HA HA HA!

"It did what?" gasped Mrs. T.

"It made her knees go wobbly," explained Ivy. "In fact, we all had knobbly wees. I mean, wobbly knees."

Mrs. Twelvetrees obviously didn't know what to say, but then Gwendoline Tutt put her hand up.

"I know what the face was," said Gwendoline. Everybody turned to look at her.

Ooooh, she looked SO pleased with herself.

"It was Mr. Motley, the custodian," she said.

"What would Mr. Motley be doing at school so late at night?" asked Mrs. Twelvetrees.

"My dad phoned him to tell him to make the

73

bell stop ringing," said Gwendoline. "It kept me awake all night, and the night before that, and the night before that . . ."

Honestly, what a fuss! She lives at number 59, which is quite a ways down Odd Street. I bet she could hardly hear it.

"Thank you, Gwendoline," said Mrs. Twelvetrees. "In that case, would somebody please fetch Mr. Motley so he can tell us himself?"

"I'll go!" I said, and whizzed off before I had to hear any more of Gwendoline Tutt's tuttishness.

Motley turned out to be in Mrs. Twelvetrees's office. He was fiddling with the glass tank on the windowsill, which is where Tony, the school turtle, lives. I told Motley that Mrs. Twelvetrees wanted him in the auditorium.

"I'm too busy," said Motley.

"Doing what?"

"Tony's tank has a leak," said Motley. "He's having a vacation in my bucket while I glue it."

Sure enough, Motley's red bucket was on the floor, and Tony was sitting in it looking very grumpy.

"I've got just the thing to cheer him up," said Motley.

He reached into his pocket and pulled out a handful of Fishpopz. He dropped a few into the bucket and shoved the rest in his mouth.

"These fishy chews are very nice, by the way," he said. "We love them, don't we, Tony?"

"Forget the Fishpopz," I said. "Mrs. Twelvetrees wants you to come and talk to everybody."

"Me?" said Motley with his mouth full. "Talk to everybody? Oh, no, I couldn't do that. What would I say?"

"She wants to know if you were at the school last night."

"Oh, dear," said Motley, chewing away. "Oh, deary dear!"

Soon me and Motley were back in the auditorium and he had to go up to the front.

"Aha! There you are, Mr. Motley," said Mrs. Twelvetrees. "Can you PLEASE tell everybody what you were doing at school last night?"

Poor Motley looked really nervous. He was a bit shy and didn't like being in front of everyone. He just shook his head.

"Come on, Mr. Motley, we won't bite you! Tell us what you were doing."

"I can't," said Motley.

"Yes, you can," said Mrs. T. "Show some gumption!"

"No, I can't," said Motley. "I wasn't at school last night."

GASP! We all looked at each other.

"He's lying!" snapped Gwendoline. "A ton of people saw you."

"How do you know what we saw?" said Martha.

"It was a green face flying around," said Ivy. "How could that be him?"

Mrs. Twelvetrees raised her hands to make us quiet down, and then she turned to Motley. "Did Mr. Tutt call to tell you to make the bell stop ringing?"

Motley looked uncomfortable. "Yes, but it stopped by itself," said Motley. "So I wasn't at school. Nowhere near school. You can't make me say that I was."

Gwendoline looked shocked — ha ha!

"There has to be a sensible explanation," said

Mrs. Twelvetrees. "Maybe Miss Barking can tell us what's going on?"

Miss Barking got a funny look on her face. She opened up her folder and shuffled through all her pieces of paper. "There's nothing here about ghosts," said Miss Barking. "And Miss Pingle's window did close by itself."

"Humph," said Mrs. T. again. She came over to where our class was sitting. "Is that the truth?"

None of us wanted to get Ivy into trouble, so we all nodded.

"Well, I'd like to see this ghost for myself," said Mrs. Twelvetrees. "So why don't we have a little fun with this? We'll have a GHOST WATCH! Anybody who wants to help has to write a ghost story, and then we'll meet here tonight. We'll tell our stories to bring the ghost out. If there IS a ghost, we'll see it, and if we don't see a ghost, then we'll know there isn't one. How's that?"

It was 10/10 UTTERLY AWESOME!

The Door in the Ceiling

After the assembly, it was recess. I wanted the others to come with me to look in the library, because that's where we'd seen the ghost in the window.

Poor Ellie started to shake. "I'm not going in there!" she said.

"Me neither," said Martha. "I'm banned from

the library. It's a pity, because those bookcases make great goalposts."

Ivy laughed. "That's why you were banned!"

So me and Ivy and Bianca set off, but first we stopped by the music room so Bianca could get her trombone.

"Why do we need that?" asked Ivy.

"If Bianca's practicing, then nobody will come in," I said.

A few minutes later, some terrifying sounds were coming out the library door.

BWARB BWEEB BOOP!

Bianca was blowing her trombone, trying to get a new high note she'd never gotten before. Anybody outside who was going past would think it was the ghost getting his finger trapped in a drawer—ha ha, awesome!

While Bianca was busy blasting away, me and Ivy had a look around.

Everything seemed perfectly normal. There were

no ghosts or balloons
with faces on them or
anything like that. We
looked up to try to fig-
ure out which part of
the window we'd seen
the face in and noticed
a square panel in the
ceiling.

"It looks like a cabinet door," said Ivy.

"A cabinet in the ceiling?" I said. "Don't be crazy.
I bet that's the way up to the clock tower."

"Let's find out!" said Ivy.

Next to the window was a big tall bookcase full
of fat books that nobody ever read. Before I could
stop her, Ivy was climbing up the shelves and the

whole thing had started to wobble! I clung to the bottom of the bookcase to hold it steady, and Ivy nearly kicked me in the eye.

"It's not safe!" I warned her.

"Don't worry, I'm fine," said Ivy, and then she stepped on my fingers.

"YOW!" I shouted, so Bianca did an extra-loud *BARROOOB* to drown me out.

Ivy grabbed the top of the bookcase with both hands, then pulled herself up with her legs flying everywhere.

"Hey, Agatha!" she said, waving down at me. "It's filthy up here. I bet nobody's cleaned it for years."

Ivy had managed to lie flat on top of the bookcase. That would have been enough for most people, but not Ivy. The next thing I knew, she was standing up. The bookcase was wobbling even more, so I had to grab on even tighter.

When Ivy reached up, she could just touch the square panel and push it up a tiny bit.

"I've done it!" she said proudly. "Hey, Agatha, if you pass me some of those big books on the bottom shelf, I could climb on them and get in there."

"No way!" I said. It was bad enough watching her as it was.

"Spoilsport," said Ivy. Then she tapped on the panel to test it for ghosts, but none came out.

By this time Bianca was going purple.

BWEEP BWURP went the trombone.

"Come on, get down," I said. "Bianca can't play much more."

Ivy started to slide off the bookcase, but then lost her grip.

"Argh!" she shouted.

I made a big mistake. I looked up and Ivy fell on me, along with a ton of dust and bent thumbtacks and old candy wrappers and DEAD SPIDERS, which all landed on my face. Yuck.

Me and Ivy brushed each other off to try to get clean.

"What's that stuck in your hair, Agatha?" asked Ivy. She pulled out a little gray wrinkled triangle. "It looks like an ancient chip."

I took it from her and gave it a sniff. "That's not a chip," I said. "I know exactly what it is!"

I'd recognize that fishy wet-dog smell anywhere.

Bianca had packed up her trombone and was standing next to Ivy. They were both staring at me.

"Agatha, you're pulling your hair!" said Ivy.

She was right—I was. It's what I always do when I'm waking my brain up. I needed to know . . . what was a Fishpopz tail doing on top of the old bookcase?

The Dark Auditorium

That night after dinner, I rounded up the others and we set off back to school in the dark for the ghost watch. It was very exciting—WOO-HOO!

The best part was that we didn't think Ellie would come, but she told us she'd written a really good ghost story and didn't want to waste it.

Even though she was scared silly, she wasn't

backing out. YO, ELLIE—WHAT A STAR! It's always better when the five of us are together.

When we got to the school gates, there was a whole bunch of other people already there, but the bad news was that they included Gwendoline and Olivia.

"Oh, look, it's Ellie Jelly-Knees!" sneered Gwendoline. "I warn you, we've got a ghost story that'll completely freak you out, don't we, Olivia?"

"Hur, hur," sniggered Olivia, which didn't sound nice, but then she never does.

When we got inside, just Motley, Mrs. Twelvetrees, and Miss Pingle were waiting for us.

Motley was holding the main door open, but once we were all in, he shut the door and locked it.

"Thank you, Mr. Motley," said Mrs. Twelvetrees. "Are you going to join us in the auditorium for the ghost watch?"

"Not me," said Motley. "I've got work to do."

We all dumped our coats in the coatroom, then went into the auditorium. It was really dark— oo-eee! All the main lights were off. There was just a little electric candle flickering away in the middle of the floor, and we had to sit around it in a circle. Me and Ellie and Martha and Ivy and Bianca all huddled together.

"Keep a sharp lookout, gang!" said Mrs. T. "Now, who's going to tell the first ghost story?"

Ivy's hand shot into the air, and she started bouncing around on her bottom.

"Oh me please let me yeah WOW me please me WOW please pleaseyplease PLEASE?"

"Golly!" said Mrs. Twelvetrees. "All right, then, Ivy. Go ahead!"

Ivy took a deep breath, then spoke in a very low

voice: "Many years ago, there was an evil school receptionist called Miss Wizzit."

HA HA HA!

Everybody laughed, but Mrs. Twelvetrees made a face. "That's not very kind," she said.

"It's not the Miss Wizzit that we have now," explained Ivy. "This is a completely different Miss Wizzit, who went nuts if you leaned your elbows on her desk when you talked to her and kept a mug full of rubber bands to zap flies and spiders with."

It sounded like our Miss Wizzit!

"Anyway," said Ivy, "this evil Miss Wizzit never let anybody use the photocopier."

It sounded *exactly* like our Miss Wizzit! But before Mrs. Twelvetrees could object, Ivy hurried on with her story.

"The evil Miss Wizzit put a dreadful curse on the photocopier so if anybody used it, something really bad would happen."

"Ooooh!" we all said.

"Then one day an evil teacher called Miss Barking . . ."

HA HA HA!

"IVY!" said Mrs. Twelvetrees. "That is not nice."

"I don't mean *our* Miss Barking," said Ivy. "I meant another Miss Barking, who kept everybody from having fun and wore silly clothes."

"That's enough, Ivy," said Mrs. Twelvetrees. "Has anybody else got a ghost story?"

"But I haven't told you about when Miss Barking used the photocopier without asking and it printed

out lots of skeletons and she was really scared," said Ivy.

"Oh, go ahead," said Mrs. T. "What happened?"

"Miss Barking used the photocopier without asking and it printed out lots of skeletons and she was really scared," said Ivy. "And that's it. The end."

WAHOO! Good one, Ivy. We all gave her a round of applause—clap, clap, clap. Even Mrs. Twelvetrees laughed.

"You see, children?" she said. "Ghosts are just for funny stories. Has anybody else got one?"

Nobody really wanted to tell a story after Ivy because she was so funny, but then Miss Pingle noticed Ellie was holding a piece of paper.

"Is that your story, Ellie?" asked Miss Pingle.

Everybody looked at Ellie, so she got all shy and tried to fold her paper away.

"Chin up, Ellie!" said Mrs. Twelvetrees. "At least tell us what it's about."

"It's about a ghost called Nosy Rosie," said Ellie.

"Goodness!" said Mrs. Twelvetrees.

We all cheered, which made Ellie feel braver. She took a deep breath and began to read aloud.

"Nosy Rosie never minded her own business

and always used to stick her nose in where it wasn't wanted. Then one time she stuck her nose around the kitchen door, and the cook grabbed a knife and chopped Rosie's nose off. Rosie screamed and picked her nose up and put it back on, but she did it so fast, she put her nose on upside down. She always hoped that nobody would notice, but there was one thing that always gave her away: whenever she sneezed, her hat blew off."

HA HA HA HA HA!

We all had a good laugh, and Ellie looked very proud. The only person who spoiled it was Gwendoline, who pretended to yawn.

"That is the stupidest story I ever heard," she said. "It isn't funny. It isn't even scary."

"That's the whole point," said Mrs. T. "Ghosts are NOT scary."

"Oh, no?" said Gwendoline. "I'll tell you a scary story. It's called 'The Crawling Hand'!" Gwendoline looked very smug.

I didn't like the sound of this.

"One time a boy was feeling really cold, so he went to hide in the school coatroom."

Typical Gwendoline. She was obviously going to make a joke about what Olivia did to Ellie. We could feel Ellie shivering, but we didn't want Gwendoline to know, so we kept quiet.

Gwendoline continued. "He wrapped himself in all the coats and then sat on the hottest radiator and then . . . he melted away to nothing! The only part left was his hand."

"Urgh!" we all said.

"And the hand still crawls around the coatroom today. If you get too close, it reaches out and GRABS YOU!"

"ARGHHHHHHHHHHH!" shrieked Ellie. "ARGHHHHHHHH!"

Suddenly Ellie was clinging to me. Behind us in the darkness, two people were having a wrestling match.

"Let me go!" shouted one of them. It was Olivia.

"What is going on?" Mrs. Twelvetrees demanded. She lifted up the electric candle. We all saw Olivia lying face-down on the floor. Martha was sitting on top of her and wasn't getting off.

"She sneaked up behind us," said Martha. "And

when Gwendoline finished her story, Olivia grabbed
Ellie to scare her."

What a rotten trick! No wonder Ellie screamed.

"Did you plan this, Gwendoline?" said Mrs.
Twelvetrees crossly.

"It has nothing to do with me," said Gwendoline innocently.

"Get this big lump off me," gasped Olivia, because Martha had squeezed all the breath out of her.

"What big lump would that be?" asked Martha. "I can't see a big lump."

"Get off, Martha, thank you," said Mrs. Twelvetrees. "And as for you, Olivia, from now on you'll sit next to me."

Martha got up and Olivia crawled around to sit by Mrs. Twelvetrees. She sat there rubbing her ribs and making a fuss and we didn't care.

"Are we telling more ghost stories?" asked Ivy.

"No," said Mrs. Twelvetrees strictly. "What we are going to do now is keep very quiet and listen.

Every time we hear a noise, we're going to figure out what it is. Ready? Then shhh . . ."

We all held our breath and listened.

There was a little creaking from high up above us.

"That's just the roof," said Mrs. Twelvetrees. "The wooden timbers are very old, and they make a little noise when they heat up or cool down or the wind blows on them."

Next we heard a car going past, so that was a bit boring.

Then we heard a strange bubbling noise followed by a few little squeaks.

"Oh, dear," said Mrs. Twelvetrees. "What can that be?"

We all laughed because we knew it was Martha's tummy rumbling.

"Sorry," said Martha. "I didn't have much for dinner tonight."

"Oh, no?" said Olivia, making a face. "I bet you had ten helpings at least."

"Shhh!" said Mrs. Twelvetrees. "Let's see what else we can hear."

"How can we see what we can hear?" asked Ivy.

"Shhhh!" said Mrs. Twelvetrees.

It was quiet for a few minutes.

But then . . . *Cullink — Clang!*

"Eeeek!" squeaked Miss Pingle. "What was that?"

It was just Motley putting his bucket down somewhere in the hall!

Slop splosh splupp!

Motley was doing some mopping.

Tooty toot toot!

It was Motley whistling a little tune. We all got the giggles.

"See?" said Mrs. Twelvetrees. "All these noises can be explained."

Suddenly the lights came on in the hall and a bright blast shone in through the auditorium door — DAZZLE, DAZZLE. It ruined the atmosphere.

"AWWW!" we all moaned.

"Miss Pingle, could you go and ask Mr. Motley if he could work with the lights off?" asked Mrs. T.

So Miss Pingle went to speak to Motley, and by the time she got back, the lights were all off again.

After that, it was quiet for a long time. Mrs. Twelvetrees looked at her watch, then finally took a deep breath.

"I think we've waited long enough," she said. "It's just a nice old building, and there is no . . ."

"ARGHHHHHH!"

A horrible scream came echoing down the hall. We all jumped out of our skin. Mrs. Twelvetrees dashed over to the door and clicked the lights on. Motley staggered into the auditorium, looking as white as a sheet.

"I saw it!" wailed Motley.

"Really?" said Mrs. T. "Where?"

"In the coatroom," said Motley. "I'd just gone in to fill my bucket up in the sink in there, and it was dark, so I was feeling around for the faucet. And then I got this horrible feeling I was being watched! So I looked around, and there it was, staring at me!"

"What was staring at you?" asked Mrs. T.

"The ghost," said Motley. "It was glowing in the dark. It was hideous."

"It must be someone playing a joke," said Mrs. T.

"That would be Olivia," said Martha.

"Yeah, she's hideous," said Ivy.

But Gwendoline and Olivia were both there. In fact, everybody was there. Nobody else had come in or gone out.

"I tell you, there was somebody else in the coatroom," said Motley. "Somebody . . . or some*thing!*"

"We'll just see about THAT," said Mrs. T. She marched over to the sports supplies cabinet and pulled out a chunky old tennis racket, then gave it a few practice swipes — *SWISH SWOTT!*

"All right, follow me!" she said. We all set off down the hall with Mrs. T. marching along in front, waving the racket around her head. "Come out, come out, whoever you are!" she shouted. Then she stomped into the coatroom.

She prodded at all the coats—PROD PROD PROD!

In the end, it was kind of boring. There weren't any zombies or skeletons or anything.

Motley was waiting out in the hall with Miss Pingle.

"You've been having too many late nights, Mr. Motley," said Miss Pingle. "You need a break."

"There WAS something there," said Motley. "All horrible and wrinkled. And ugly." Motley was looking a bit wobbly.

Me and Martha took hold of his arms to steady him.

"We'll help him down to his office," I said. "Don't worry, Mr. Motley, we'll look after you."

"Good plan," said Mrs. T., coming out of the coatroom. "And in the meantime, we'll check the rest of the school. Follow me, gang!"

Off she went, waving her tennis racket, and everybody followed her, shouting, "Come out, come out, wherever you are!"

Poor little ghost! All it wanted to do was drift around making a few ghostie faces. It didn't need to be whacked into ghost fries by Mrs. Twelvetrees with a tennis racket. I was starting to feel quite sorry for it.

The THING in Motley's office

If you go down to the school basement, there's a door with a sign on it that says WARNING! KEEP OUT! DANGER!

You're getting all excited now, aren't you? I remember the first time I saw it. I thought it'd be like a mad science laboratory with big blue electric sparks zapping across the roof and chopped-off heads in jars with their mouths moving and stuff like that. AWESOME!

Don't get your hopes up. The sign is a big lie. It's actually the storeroom for all the old school junk, like soccer nets, broken musical instruments, and costumes from school plays. There's also a table with a kettle and tea stuff on it, and a battered old arm-chair. The only thing that might be a teeny bit dangerous is the half bottle of milk that has probably been sitting

there for 150 years and is turning blue around the edges.

Welcome to Motley's office! This is where he comes for a nice little nap while we're all stuck upstairs learning 4 x 7 = 28 and all that stuff.

UNFAIR.

Motley was still shaking a little when me and Martha got him into his chair. His kettle and his cookies were on the table, and next to them was a Fishpopz box.

"I'll have some of these fishy chews," said Motley. "That'll steady my nerves."

He shoved his hand in the box, but it was empty.

"Oh, dear," he said. "I must have finished them. Pity. They were nice."

"Never mind Fishpopz," I said. "What you need is a cup of tea."

"And some cookies," said Martha. Then she ate one just to test it.

I put a tea bag in Motley's mug, but the kettle wasn't plugged in. There was a row of sockets, but they were all being used. One wire was running off to a lumpy black thing sitting in Motley's red bucket.

"What's this?" asked Martha.

"It's a heater for Tony," said Motley.

"But he's not in here," said Martha, looking in the bucket.

"I know," said Motley. "I had to put him somewhere else. I needed my bucket for mopping."

Motley reached over to the sockets to unplug Tony's heater and suddenly everything went black . . . and that's when we saw it.

EEEEK!

Actually, we didn't shout—we were so freaked, we couldn't breathe or even make a noise. The ghost was there, right in front of us, glowing in the dark!

"Sorry," said the ghost. "I must have unplugged the light. Hang on, I'll get it back."

The light came back on. There was Motley, looking perfectly normal again.

"Motley, is that really you?" I asked.

"Of course it's me," said Motley.

I turned to Martha. "It looks like Motley, and it sounds like Motley."

Martha gave Motley a prod in the ribs.

"It feels like Motley," said Martha.

"What was that for?" asked Motley, rubbing where Martha prodded, because Martha prods quite hard.

"Answer me one question," I said. "Which is your favorite bucket?"

"My red one, of course!" said Motley, and a big warm smile flashed across his face. "We're old friends, me and that bucket. We can even do a magic trick together."

Martha and me looked at each other. "It IS Motley!" we said. Of course it was. There was only one person in the universe who loved buckets as much as Motley. (If you want to know about Motley's bucket trick, it's on page 145.)

"Did you know your head glows in the dark?" I asked.

"It does WHAT?" said Motley.

So we showed him.

In a corner of the basement was the props box where they keep all the stuff from the school plays. Last year Miss Bunn's class did *Sleeping Beauty*, so I went and dug out the magic mirror.

I held it up in front of Motley, and then Martha turned the light off.

"Oh, dear!" said Motley, looking at the greeny-white head glowing in the mirror. "Is that really me?"

"That's you," I said. "By day you are kindly Mr. Motley, the school custodian. But when night falls, you are . . . the Odd Street School Ghost!"

"But what was that horrible thing I saw upstairs?" said Motley.

"It was your reflection in the coatroom mirror!" I said.

Motley stared at his green head a bit more, then made a few faces and winked at himself.

"Actually, I was wrong," he said. "This ghost isn't horrible at all. In fact, I'd say it's rather handsome."

Ha ha ha!

"So why are you glowing?" asked Martha.

"Just a natural talent, I suppose," said Motley.

But then we noticed some glowing dots on the floor. I picked one up, and Martha turned the light on to see what it was.

"It's one of those Fishpopz," I said. "There must be something in them that makes you glow in the dark."

"Ha ha!" Martha laughed. "No wonder Mrs. Twelvetrees didn't find anybody else in the coat-room."

"I feel like a bit of a fool," admitted Motley. "You won't tell anyone, will you?"

"Of course not," I said. "But what about the ghost we all saw last night?"

"You said it wasn't you," said Martha.

Motley got very quiet and made a little guilty face.

"It *was* you, wasn't it, Motley?" I said. "You were going up to the clock tower to make the bell stop ringing."

"Isn't there a switch to turn it off in the office?" asked Martha.

Motley shook his head. "It's clockwork," he said. "There is a switch, but that's just to wind it up. The only way to keep it from ringing is to get up there."

"But Miss Barking has locked up the ladder!" I said. "So Motley had to climb the bookcase. And he dropped a bit of Fishpopz on the top."

At last, it all made sense. Motley had gone up to stop the bell, and we had seen him climbing down. Then he must have lost his grip and slipped and shouted out, just like Ivy did!

"But why was he in the dark?" said Martha.

"If he turned the lights on and somebody saw him through the window, he'd have been in trouble!" I said. Then I gave Motley my HARD STARE. "Well? That's right, isn't it, Motley?"

Motley nodded. "Mr. Tutt said I'd lose my job if I didn't stop the bell," said Motley. "And Miss Barking said I'd lose my job if I climbed on the furniture."

"We don't want you to lose your job, Motley!" we both said.

"So you promise you won't tell?" said Motley.

"Of course!" We nodded, and to seal the deal, he gave us both another cookie.

Martha was just about to swallow her cookie in one bite when she paused and put her finger to her lips. She'd heard something outside the door. Very quietly she went over and pulled it open. Gwendoline was there!

"Well, this is very cozy, isn't it?" said Gwendoline. "Keeping little secrets, are we?"

"Have you been listening?" demanded Martha.

"I just want to know why Motley is going to lose his job," said Gwendoline. "Is it for pretending to be a ghost? Well, he doesn't scare me!"

"He wasn't pretending anything," I said.

"Oh, so you're telling me there's a REAL ghost, are you?" sneered Gwendoline.

"Yes, I am!" I said. "But it isn't Motley. It's NOSY ROSIE!"

Gwendoline's big mouth dropped open in shock. "Nosy Rosie?" She gasped.

"That's right. Ellie was telling the truth, so you better watch out, Gwendoline!"

"You're pathetic, Agatha," said Gwendoline. "Really, I mean it. SO pathetic."

Then she went away—THANK GOODNESS.

"What did you say that for?" asked Martha.

"I couldn't stop myself," I said. "Gwendoline really bugs me, and then I remembered I'd seen a mask in the props box."

"And . . . ?" said Martha.

"I got this silly idea," I said. "We chop off the nose and turn it upside down. Then we cover the mask in Fishpopz to make it glow. Then one of us puts it on with a hat and waits in the dark for Gwendoline."

"That is AWESOME!" said Martha. "Oh, please, let me do it! Please?"

To be honest, I thought it was so silly, I wished I

hadn't mentioned it, but Martha was already looking through the props box and Motley was collect-
ing the loose Fishpopz off the floor.

One minute later, Martha was dressed up and
ready, so we switched the light off. It was really
freaky! All you could see was the green face and the
hat. It didn't look like Martha at all.

Next to me, Motley was still glowing too, or at least I hoped it was Motley! People look very different when their heads light up. And that's true.

"Okay, Martha," I said. "Sneeze and throw your hat off."

"Aah-tishoo!" went Martha, and then something hit me in the face.

EEEK!

Even though I knew Martha had tossed the hat at me, it was a lot creepier than I'd thought it would be.

Just as we turned the light back on, Mrs. Twelvetrees shouted down the stairs.

"All clear!" she said. "Come on out—it's quite safe."

Martha took the mask off and slipped it under her shirt.

"You sneak around to the kitchen," I said. "I'll arrange for Gwendoline to come and find you."

"I'll go first and make sure the lights are off." Motley grinned. "Good luck!"

Nosy Rosie Gets a Helping Hand

Everybody was in the office getting ready to go home while Motley went around the rest of the school, turning the lights off.

The only person missing was Martha, so I told Ellie and Ivy and Bianca what she was up to, because I didn't want them to be freaked out. Of course Gwendoline came over, demanding to know what we were whispering about.

"I warned you," I said. "Don't forget what happened to Nosy Rosie."

"You don't scare me," sneered Gwendoline.

"Suit yourself," I said. "But you wouldn't catch me walking past the kitchen at this time of night. Not in the dark."

"Why not?" asked Gwendoline.

"That's where Nosy Rosie got her nose cut off," said Ellie.

"Gwendoline's pretending she's not scared," said Ivy.

"That's because I'm NOT!" said Gwendoline.

"We don't believe you," said Ivy. "Scared, scared, scared!"

"Just watch me!" said Gwendoline, and she went off down the dark hall.

We all held our breath, waiting for her to scream. It was going to be SO fabulous, especially after what Gwendoline had done to Ellie! Just for once, it would be nice to see the smug smile wiped off her face . . . but then Martha came running up the other way.

"Agatha, we left the hat downstairs!"

Oh, drat! I KNEW it had been a silly idea.

Gwendoline came back down the hall, laughing.

"So what was all that about, Agatha?" she said. "I thought you were going to have someone up there to shout 'WOOO!' or something. Like I said, you're pathetic."

What a ROTTEN way to end the night. URGHHHH. I was really mad at myself.

"Come along, gang," said Mrs. T. "Let's go home and leave Mr. Motley to lock up."

"Hang on," said Gwendoline. "I've left my coat in the coatroom."

"But it's dark," said Mrs. T.

"Do I look scared?" said Gwendoline.

So Gwendoline dashed back to the coatroom and then . . .

"ARGHHHH!"

Gwendoline came screaming back out of the darkness. "It's in there! I SAW it!"

She was completely babbling, and her eyes were like tennis balls!

"Do you mean the ghost?" Mrs. Twelvetrees demanded.

"NO!" yelled Gwendoline. "The crawling HAND! It was trying to climb out of a sink . . . and it had horrible little stumpy fingers glowing in the dark! ARGHHHH!"

She pushed past Mrs. Twelvetrees, shot out the door, and disappeared up Odd Street, still screaming her head off.

AWESOME!

And that's where this chapter ends, so you can shut the book now and save the rest until tomorrow. Tum tee tum.

Nice and relaxed, are you? Excellent.

Or are you still wondering what the crawling hand was? If so, don't worry, because I'll tell you in the next chapter. I wasn't going to tell ANYONE, but the old man who types these books out for me said you might have nightmares, and I don't want that! In fact, you can read the next chapter now, if you want to. It's only a little shortie.

The Little Shortie Chapter

After Gwendoline ran off screaming, we were all left standing by the door, feeling completely freaked out. Even Mrs. Twelvetrees looked a bit unstable.

Just then the lights came on in the hall, and Motley came around the corner, carrying his bucket.

"Is everything all right?" asked Motley. "I heard some shouting in the coatroom, so I went to take a look."

"Thank you, Mr. Motley," said Mrs. Twelvetrees. "Tell us, did you happen to see a crawling hand?"

"No," said Motley. "I'm sure I'd remember if I had."

"Just as I thought," said Mrs. Twelvetrees, and then she spoke to us all. "Gwendoline has been playing another one of her little jokes. There are NO ghosts, so off you go, girls. See you all tomorrow!"

But we knew Gwendoline hadn't been joking. Her jokes always involved upsetting other people, not herself!

Motley held the door open for us to leave. I wondered if it had been one of HIS hands crawling around, but they both seemed to be fixed onto his arms pretty solidly, so it couldn't have been that.

But then as I walked past, I looked into his red bucket. There was a grumpy little face looking back up at me, chewing on a Fishpopz.

"I see you've got Tony back," I said.

"Yes, I'd left him in one of the sinks so he could have a swim," said Motley.

Good grief! Tony was about the same size as a hand, and his little legs and his head could have looked like stumpy fingers . . . and he'd been eating Fishpopz!

"So what do you think that hand was all about?" asked Motley.

"No idea," I said. "No idea at all." And I didn't tell ANYBODY!

(Well, apart from you, of course. Oh, and I had to tell Ellie because I didn't want her to be frightened anymore, and I told Martha because I wanted to make up for my stupid mask idea. And I told Ivy because if she found out I knew and hadn't told her, she'd tickle me to death—OW OOOH HA HA NO STOPPIT—and I told Bianca because if I hadn't told her, Ivy would have told her, but aside from that, I did not tell anybody, ESPECIALLY NOT GWENDOLINE.)

The Last DONG!

When I got home, it was quite late. James and Tilly were already in bed, and Mom was taking a long bath. Dad asked if we'd seen the ghost again, but I was keeping quiet about Motley, so I said no. Then he asked if I wanted a snack.

"Don't tell your mom," he whispered. "Look what I got!"

It was a HUGE pink box with a picture of an

alien on the front with two heads and long octopus arms sticking out.

"It's Space Munch!" he said.

"From Spendless?" I asked.

Dad nodded. "Special sale."

"No way," I said.

"Oh, come on," said Dad. "It can't be as bad as that last stuff."

But sure enough, he tried a bit, and chewed it and chewed it.

"I give up," said Dad. "Maybe Mr. Motley wants it?"

Hmm. I looked at the picture on the box and tried to imagine Motley with two heads and octopus arms. Not pretty.

"I don't think we'll risk it!" I said.

So up I went to bed, and that was the end of that. I must have gone straight to sleep, because before I knew it, there was a great big . . .

DONG!

I'd forgotten. A man had come to fix the

school clock that afternoon, and he'd brought his own ladder!

DONG!

Everything else was completely quiet, so I guessed it was midnight.

DONG!

I had to laugh because I knew Bianca, Martha, Ivy, and Ellie would all be lying awake listening and counting too!

DONG!

The bell was ringing perfectly. It made me feel a little sad, actually.

DONG!

It had been quite nice to think there was a ghost in the old school.

DONG!

After all, it didn't hurt anybody, and we'd all had a good laugh!

DONG!

That was the seventh *DONG,* and it wasn't very exciting.

DONG!

I knew exactly when the next *DONG* would come, and it was now . . .

DONG!

See? Where's the fun in that? Sorry, old clock, you've become boring.

DONG!

That was number ten. YAWN! Just two more to go, then that's the end of the story.

DONG!

Thanks for reading about our ghost. I hope it didn't scare you, but if it did, don't worry! We're just about to finish with one last . . .

DONG!

There, that was it. There is no more. Good night, GOODBYEEEE, and have sweet dreams because this is

THE END.

DONG!

. . . Or is it?

WOOOO!

Motley's Magic Bucket Trick

(Wahoo! We love it.)

How can you have a bucket of water upside down over your head and not get wet?

This is really freaky, because the bucket doesn't have a lid on it or anything like that! Motley showed me this with his big red bucket, but if you have a small plastic bucket, you can try it yourself.

Put a little bit of water in the bucket, then hold it by the handle.

Start to swing the bucket back and forth, with bigger and bigger swings.

Warning: You have to DO THIS OUTSIDE with lots of space around you; otherwise, you might whack the TV or your mom or your dog or something.

When you're feeling brave, give it a great BIG swing so it goes right around upside down over the top of your head. If you do it fast enough, the water stays inside!

Here's the good part. One time James was doing this trick, and he wanted me to take a photo! I got the camera ready, then when the bucket was going over his head, I told him to hold it a second while I pushed the button. So he stopped the bucket, and the water all fell out— *SPLOOSH*. It was the best photo I ever took—HA HA, awesome! The only time James was more embarrassed was when he got an email full of kisses from a mystery girl . . . but we've run out of pages now, so I'll tell you about that in another book. And that's a definite promise! xo